Stop, Thief!

FRANKLIN WATTS
LONDON•SYDNEY

1

Best of friends

Ethel Mackley and Annie Gresham sat at a long table amidst piles of feathers and ribbons and sewed in silence.

At one end of the table, a selection of unfinished hats and bonnets waited in drab brown rows.

At the other end, beautiful creations of satin and velvet sat waiting to be wrapped in tissue paper and laid in big boxes.

Ethel and Annie made hats for Mrs. Baggs of Baggs Bonnet Makers, Covent Garden. Although the two girls weren't talking, the silence wasn't uncomfortable. Ethel and Annie were the best of friends.

Annie came from the Kent countryside. Her father was a dairyman and her mother made butter and cheese to take to market. Annie had a round chubby face

with black curly hair.

Annie loved the country and not a day went by when she didn't dream of going home.

While Annie was round and rosy-cheeked, Ethel was pale with a delicate heart-shaped face. Ethel lived in a small flat in North London. Ethel's father, Arthur, was a policeman. His pay was poor and the job demanded long hours and a good record for catching criminals.

Times were hard in Ethel's house and

her mother was finding it difficult to make ends meet. There had been a string of burglaries in Belgravia where her father patrolled and still no-one had been arrested. Ethel knew that if the culprits weren't caught soon her father would not get the promotion and pay rise he was counting on.

Annie let her dark eyes see beyond the greasy glass of the front room window.

In her mind, she travelled beyond the street, beyond London and out into the sunny green fields around her parent's cottage. She took a deep breath and sighed heavily.

Across the table

Ethel put down the cap she was edging with lace.

"Thinking about home?" she asked kindly.

Annie nodded.

More and more Annie was unhappy living in her Aunt and Uncle's house. Something strange was going on there and she didn't like it. Even her little cousin, Teddy, had become edgy and secretive. He slept during the day and went out with his father at night.

Annie bit her lip as she remembered what had happened late last night. She had slipped out of her room for a drink of water. At the end of the corridor Aunt

Madge was unlocking the door to a room
Annie had been forbidden to go near.
Beside Aunt Madge stood
an evil-looking man
holding a lumpy
sack. Before
they saw her,
Annie hid
behind a curtain.

"Wotcher
got?" Aunt
Madge's
voice had
been harsh
and slurred
with gin.

The door to the mysterious room was
open. Annie could see the man standing in
front of a table. There were clanks and
thuds as he emptied the sack.

"Ten guineash," muttered Aunt Madge a few minutes later. "Take it or leave it."

"You drive a hard bargain," said the man angrily.

"Take it or leave it," she said again.

There was jingle of coins and the door slammed.

Annie pressed herself flat against the wall. She prayed that the light in the corridor was gloomy enough to hide her feet peeking out from the bottom of the curtain.

"If you want more, get the real stuff," snarled Aunt Madge as two sets of boots clumped down the stairs. In that moment Annie darted back to her bed, pulled the covers over her head and wished more than anything that she was back at home.

Now in Mrs. Baggs' front room, she looked into Ethel's pale worried face and fought back the tears that prickled at her eyes.

"I miss home," she said simply.

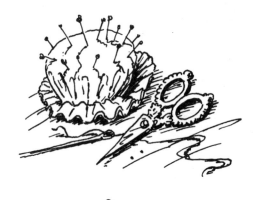

2

Strange goings-on

"Stuff and rubbish," creaked a voice like a rusty spring. "You'd never 'ave earned a livin' in that rabbit hole."

A dumpy beady-eyed woman appeared in the room. She had a face like old squirrel. Her thin reddish hair was piled on

top of her head and her bristly face was scabby and grey.

Ethel felt her stomach go cold. You never knew when Mrs. Baggs would appear. She had eyes and ears everywhere. Annie and Ethel had learned long ago to be careful what they said.

Mrs. Baggs pinched Annie on the cheek and picked up the bonnet she was sewing.

"An' yer a clever girl with a needle."

"Thank you, Mrs. Baggs," murmured Annie without taking her eyes from the table.

Ethel could see a red mark already

appearing on her friend's cheek.

Mrs. Baggs pulled a respectable woollen coat over her shabby dress.

"'Ow do I look, girls?" she asked with a gap-toothed smile. "Fancy enough for them fancy houses?"

"More like an old squirrel than ever," said Ethel to herself.

"Very fetching, Mrs. Baggs," said Ethel out loud. "Are you going visiting?"

"In a manner of speaking, Ethel." Mrs. Baggs peered at her reflection in the mirror and tweaked a long curly whisker from her chin.

"I'm delivering one of your bonnets to Lady Eloise Everington."

"Will you take tea with Lady Eloise?" asked Annie.

Mrs. Baggs lifted a gorgeous green satin bonnet from its box and turned it in her hand.

"If I have time," she replied in snooty voice. "She did invite me in last time when I went to see her to do the fitting."

"What is her house like?" asked Annie.

"That's none of yer business," snapped Mrs. Baggs, her voice rising suddenly. "Just you stay here till I come back."

"Yes, Mrs. Baggs," said Ethel quietly.

"And don't answer the door no matter what."

"No, Mrs. Baggs," murmured Annie.

"Good girls," said Mrs. Baggs. Her voice softened as suddenly as it rose. Then she put the hat back in its box and stumped out of the room.

A moment later the front door slammed.

"Has she gone?" asked Ethel. Sometimes Mrs. Baggs just pretended to leave the house.

Annie stood up and watched the dumpy figure of Mrs. Baggs disappear down the street.

"Yes," she said.

Then she put her bonnet on the table and burst into tears.

"Ethel," she sobbed. "There's something wrong

going on at my Aunt and Uncle's house. I
don't know what to do."

★ ★ ★

Annie had barely finished telling Ethel
about what had happened the night before
when there was a terrible pounding on the
front door.

"Open up! Open up!"

The two girls threw down their sewing
and ran along the corridor.

"What are we going
to do?" whispered
Annie. "Mrs. Baggs
will beat us if we let
anyone in."

"I know yer there!"
shouted a voice. It
was high and
squeaky. It sounded
like a young boy.

"Mrs. Baggs said so herself."

Annie and Ethel stared at each other in astonishment.

"Open up!" called the voice. "Mrs. Baggs' orders!"

"We're not opening the door until you tell us you who you are," cried Ethel, surprised at her own fierceness. "Them's Mrs. Baggs' orders, too!"

"Mrs. Baggs 'as 'ad a fall," shouted the boy. "She said if you don't open this door, she'll have your heads for pin cushions."

Ethel and Annie looked at each. It was an expression Mrs. Baggs used all the time and she normally poked you with a pin as she said it.

Ethel lifted the big key from its hook and opened the door.

3

A special delivery

A young boy stood on the doorstep. His
clothes were filthy and his feet were bare
and covered in sores. In his grubby hands,
he held the round blue hat box that Mrs.
Baggs had picked up barely twenty
minutes earlier.

Ethel stared in the boy's grimy face.

"Where's Mrs. Baggs and what are you doing with that box?"

"You Ethel?" asked the boy.

"I might be" said Ethel. The boy held out the box.

"You're to deliver this," he said. "The one called Annie's to stay 'ere."

"How do we know you're telling the truth?" asked Annie. "Where is Mrs. Baggs?"

"With the washerwoman in Bay Street," replied the boy. "She slipped in the mud and twisted her ankle. The washerwoman's wrapped it for 'er."

The boy pushed the hat box into

Ethel's hands.

"There's a penny under the china dog in the parlour. Mrs. Baggs says you're to fetch it for me."

"I think he's telling the truth," whispered Annie.

"So do I," muttered Ethel. She set the hat box down carefully on the floor.

"You wait here." And before the boy could push his way in, she slammed the door in his face.

Annie turned the handle of the parlour door. It was a room Mrs. Baggs never let them see.

At first sight, there was nothing strange about Mrs. Baggs's parlour. The air was

heavy with mothballs and it was dark
because the curtains were drawn. Annie
pulled them open to let in some light.

Sure enough there was a china dog on
the mantelpiece and a penny underneath
it, as the boy had said.

Then, as Annie drew the curtain
again, she noticed the newspaper article
about Lady Eloise Everington.

It was the same one her Aunt Madge had been reading the night before. It was on top of a pile of newspapers half pushed behind a chair.

Annie bent down. Each paper was folded open at a story about a fashionable London house and the people that lived in it. The names had been underlined and so had the addresses.

Annie looked again at the story about Lady Eloise Everington. The family was famous for its collection of silver and Lady Eloise was a leading London hostess.

The address, 23 Lexington Square, was underlined in black.

Annie felt her stomach go cold even though she wasn't sure why.

"Ethel -" she began.

At that moment, the pounding started again.

"I want my money," shouted the boy.

"I'd better be off myself," said Ethel and the two of them hurried from the room.

4

The silver swallow

Half an hour later, Ethel walked into a leafy square surrounded by huge houses. She had tidied herself up as much as she could and Annie had quickly trimmed a plain bonnet with leftover blue ribbon.

Ethel took a deep breath and walked

up the spotless granite steps of Number 23. It wasn't until she pulled back the gleaming brass knocker, that it occurred to her to wonder how Annie had known Lady Eloise's address.

The huge black door opened a fraction and a snooty footman with a face like a rat appeared.

"Round the back for the likes of you."

Ethel stared at him.

"I beg your pardon."

"Round the back," snapped the footman again. The door began to close.

"I have come

to see Lady Eloise Everington," said Ethel firmly. "I have strict instructions to deliver this parcel to her in person."

"Lady Eloise's out."

"Who's at the door, Burton?" called a rich deep voice.

A beautiful red-haired woman appeared at the door. She had the greenest eyes Ethel had ever seen.

"You must be from Mrs. Baggs," she said looking at the hat box. "Come in. I was expecting her this morning."

"Mrs. Baggs has had a fall," explained Ethel.

"Gracious!" cried Lady Eloise. "I do hope it's not serious."

"Just a twisted ankle," said Ethel. She put the hat box on the table. "She asked me to bring you this in person."

"How very thoughtful of her. I was hoping the bonnet would be ready today." She nodded at the footman. "Please give this to the maid to take to my dressing room, Burton."

The footman bowed. "Yes, your ladyship."

Ethel knew it was rude to stare at her surroundings. But she found herself

looking at a small silver statue of a
swallow on the hall mantel. It was the
loveliest thing she had ever seen.

"Exquisite, isn't it?" murmured Lady
Eloise. "My husband gave it to me as a
wedding present."

Ethel blushed.

"I'm sorry, I didn't mean to stare."

Lady Eloise smiled.

"Don't be sorry, my dear, you have
excellent taste."

Then she opened
the front door herself
and pressed a shilling
into Ethel's hand.

Ethel skipped
down the front steps,
her mind swimming
with all the gorgeous
things she had seen.

How wonderful it must be to work in such a place and for someone as beautiful as Lady Eloise!

"Penny for your thoughts, lass!" said a kind northern voice.

"Father!" Ethel stopped and kissed the moustached face of the policeman in front of her.

"What are you doing here?"

"This is my beat, Ethel," replied Arthur Mackley, looking around at all the lovely houses. "This is Belgravia."

Ethel's eyes went wide.

"You mean, this is where all the robberies have happened?"

Her father's face turned grey and tired.

"Every other mansion in this square."

Sergeant Mackley shook his head.

"It's almost as if they all had something in common," he muttered, half to himself. "But I can't think for the life of me what it could be."

"I've just delivered my best ever bonnet to Lady Eloise Everington," said Ethel, proudly. She showed her father the shilling. "Look what she gave me."

"They're a fine family, the Everingtons," said Arthur Mackley. He winked at his daughter. "Especially at Christmas to poor policemen!"

Ethel frowned.

"I hope you catch those thieves before they rob Lady Eloise."

Arthur Mackley folded his daughter's fingers over her shiny shilling.

"So do I, lass. So do I."

5

The forbidden room

Ethel's mother put a mug of sweet tea into Annie's hand.

"Drink it, dear," she whispered. "It will make you feel better."

It was four o'clock in the morning and still dark. Annie Gresham sat in the

Mackleys' kitchen, her nightgown peeping
out from under her coat.

"Now there young Annie," said Arthur
Mackley in a kind voice. "Take a deep
breath and tell us in your own time exactly
what happened."

Annie pushed back her tangled hair.
As she spoke, she realized that her Aunt

and Uncle probably didn't even know she was gone.

"I heard them come back late again" she began in a trembling voice. "Uncle Bob and Teddy. Uncle Bob was carrying a big sack and Teddy was covered in soot."

"What made you run away?" asked Ethel gently.

Annie rubbed her tear-stained face.

"Remember I told you about the locked room."

Ethel nodded.

"As they came up the stairs, Teddy started to cry. He said he wasn't going down any more chimneys or opening any more back doors. Then Uncle shouted, 'You'll do what I say or I'll cuff ya!' Then Aunt yelled at them both to shut up."

Annie closed her eyes and saw again what had happened next.

As Uncle Bob had stomped up the stairs, he tripped and something fell out of his sack.

At the same moment Aunt Madge was unlocking the door to the mysterious room and she dropped the gin bottle she was holding.

In the crash of glass, neither of them noticed the shiny silver object that bounced to the bottom of the stairs.

Annie had waited until the door closed. Then she ran down and picked it up.

Now she reached into her coat and put the object on the table.

"I just know it's been stolen from somewhere, Sergeant Mackley," she cried. "And I don't want to be blamed."

Ethel gasped and put her hand to her mouth.

It was the beautiful silver swallow she had seen that afternoon!

"What's wrong, lass?" asked her father.

"It's the swallow I saw at Lady Eloise's house," said Ethel in a choked voice. "It was on the mantel in the front hall."

Arthur Mackley stared at the silver statue on his kitchen table. His mind echoed with the Detective Inspector's last words that afternoon – "One more unsolved burglary, Mackley and you can forget the promotion and pay rise."

Sergeant Mackley looked into his wife's

worried face. They both knew this could be the break he was hoping for. If only he could catch the culprits in time.

Sergeant Mackley put his hand on Annie's arm.

"Will you help me arrest them, lass?" he said at last.

"What will happen to Teddy?" sobbed Annie. "He's only eight!"

"Don't you worry about Teddy," replied Sergeant Mackley. "We'll take care of him." He paused. "But it'll mean jail for your Aunt and Uncle."

"They're thieves," mumbled Annie miserably. Then she sat up and finished her tea. "If you want evidence, we'd better be going, Sergeant Mackley," she said. "Whatever goes into that room doesn't stay for long."

"We'll need Lady Eloise to say the swallow is hers, father," cried Ethel.

"And all the other stuff that's been stolen," muttered Annie.

"Do you think she'd come with us?" asked Sergeant Mackley.

Ethel's eyes were wide as saucers.

"I'm sure she would, father. I'll show her the swallow and explain everything to her."

6

No time to lose!

The sun was barely rising when Sergeant Mackley, Ethel and Annie walked up the steps to Number 23 Lexington Square.

Sergeant Mackley knocked loudly on the front door.

A moment later, a sleepy-faced

manservant stood in front of them, holding
a candelabra.

Sergeant
Mackley stepped
forward.

"This is an
emergency, sir," he
cried. "Summon
your mistress
immediately!"

"That's out of
the question,"
replied the man. "Be
off with you or I'll
call the police."

"I am the
police!" replied Sergeant Mackley. He
pushed the man aside and took the
candelabra from his hands.

"Look!" cried Sergeant Mackley.

The light from the candles lit up the drawing room. Ornaments lay all over the

floor. Drawers were emptied and boxes were tipped upside down.

The manservant gasped.

"Now do you understand?" demanded Sergeant Mackley. "Fetch your mistress immediately."

"There will be no need for that!"

Lady Eloise came down the front

stairs. Her eyes were blazing and she held
a poker in her hand.

Sergeant
Mackley stepped
forward.

"I am a
policeman, your
ladyship," he said.
Once again he held
the candlesticks
high.

Lady Eloise
stopped.

"How did you
know we had been
robbed?" she cried.

"Lady Eloise," said Sergeant Mackley.
"There is no time to lose. We need your
help to catch these villains."

But Lady Eloise wasn't listening. Her

eyes went straight to the mantel in the front hall.

"My swallow! Where is my swallow?"

Ethel took the swallow from Annie and held it up to the light.

"I have it, Lady Eloise," she said "It's what's led us to you."

Lady Eloise stepped into the front hall and stared into Ethel's face.

"I recognize you," she said simply.

"You came here yesterday."

"This is my father, Lady Eloise," replied Ethel.

Lady Eloise turned to Sergeant Mackley.

"How can I help you, sir?" she said in a low determined voice.

7

An honourable service

Ten minutes later, Sergeant Mackley helped Lady Eloise, Ethel and Annie into a Hansom cab and they hurriedly set off across London.

They stopped once at the police station where Sergeant Mackley spoke briefly with the Detective Inspector.

As the cab turned into the street where Annie's Aunt and Uncle lived, Ethel stared

at the tall woman sitting opposite her.

Lady Eloise's beautiful face was hidden under a tattered hood and cloak that she had found in an old dressing-up box. Her soft kid slippers were covered in mud.

"We'd better walk from here, Sergeant Mackley," whispered Annie. "Folks notice the squeak of a cab's wheels and the sound of the horse's hooves."

The plan was simple. Annie was to slip into her Aunt's room and take the key to the forbidden room.

When Lady Eloise had identified her property she was to signal Sergeant Mackley who would then blow his whistle. Policemen from his station were already on their way.

Annie turned the handle of the front door.

"Are you sure they'll be asleep?" whispered Ethel.

Annie pulled a face.

"Dead drunk, more like."

She opened the door slowly.

An old squirrely face peered out at them.

It was Mrs. Baggs!

Lady Eloise's tattered hood and cloak didn't fool Mrs. Baggs for a second.

She opened her mouth to shout but Sergeant Mackley moved as fast as a fox and clamped his hand around her mouth.

Ethel stared dumbly at Mrs. Baggs's squirming figure. What was she doing here?

"Quick, lass," whispered Sergeant Mackley to Annie. "Show Lady Eloise the room."

Annie raced up the stairs and tiptoed into her Aunt's bedroom.

Ethel could hear the snores from the corridor.

A moment later the door to the forbidden room was open.

Lady Eloise gasped.

Ethel and Annie couldn't believe their eyes!

The room looked like a treasure trove. Silver plates and ornaments were stacked everywhere.

And it all came from 23 Lexington Square!

Lady Eloise stood at the top of stairs and held up her hand.

It was the signal Arthur Mackley was waiting for.

He blew his whistle as hard as he could!

★ ★ ★

"Baggs was in on it too!!" screamed Aunt Madge as she was carried downstairs by two burly policeman. "'Oo d'ya think told us what to steal?"

Suddenly Sergeant Mackley remembered what Annie had said about the newspaper articles in Mrs. Baggs's parlour! Of course! Mrs. Baggs was the missing piece of the puzzle! She was the one who delivered the hats in person. She was the one who snooped around inside. The one who chose which house to rob next!

He looked at Annie and remembered about the newspaper article she had seen

in her Aunt's house
as well.

At that moment,
a sooty-faced boy ran
down the stairs and out
the front door.

"Stop, thief!"
bellowed a policeman
and set off after him.

"He's not a thief," screamed
Annie.

Sergeant Mackley put a firm hand on
Annie's shoulder.

"He mustn't get away, lass," he said.
"If he escapes, we can't help him."

It was too much for Annie. She
slumped against the wall and began
to sob.

★ ★ ★

The sun was high in the sky.

Ethel stood with her father and Lady Eloise as Annie and Teddy climbed into the stagecoach that would take them home to Kent.

Lady Eloise had arranged everything. She had even given Annie a small allowance to send Teddy back to school.

Ethel waved so hard she thought her hand would drop off. It was the only way

to stop herself from crying.

"I'm grateful for your help, Annie lass," said Arthur Mackley, gruffly. "I'd never have got my promotion without you."

Annie rubbed at her eyes.

"I can put care of Inspector Mackley on my letters, now," Annie cried, managing a smile. "That will sound posh!"

Ethel grabbed her friend's hand for the

last time.

"And I will write and tell you everything, every day! I promise!"

"Everything? asked Lady Eloise, kindly. "That will be a very long letter, my dear, because you will be very, very busy working for me!"

As the coach rumbled down the cobbled road, Inspector Mackley put his arms around his daughter's shoulder.

"You have made us all very happy, Lady Eloise," he said in his gentle northern voice.

"It is you who have made me happy," replied Lady Eloise Everington. "Without your help, I would have lost my beloved swallow." She winked at Ethel. "And I would never have found my charming new maid."

Ethel went scarlet. She had never felt

so sad and happy all at once.

Lady Eloise held out her gloved hand.

"It's policemen like you, Inspector Mackley, that make it possible for people like me to live safely in London."

Now it was Arthur Mackley's turn to blush.

"Thank you, ma'am."

"Thank you, Inspector Mackley." Lady Eloise's clear green eyes shone brighter than ever. "I am honoured to have been of service to you."

Notes

The London Police Force

The London Police Force
was set up in 1829 by Sir
Robert Peel who was
Home Secretary at that
time. The first policemen
were called 'Peelers'.
They wore top hats
instead of helmets
so that the public
didn't think of
them as a
military force.

Child labour

Full-time education for children was not
compulsory until the middle of the
nineteenth century. Before then thousands

of children were virtual slaves working in factories and in 'sweat shops' making garments.

Dress code

In Victorian times, middle-class women never went outside without wearing a hat or bonnet. Different kinds of bonnets were worn at different times of day. Lacy caps were often worn inside the house.